Leila Aboulela is an award-winning writer whose work has received praise for its exploration of identity, migration and Islamic spirituality. Her most recent novel, *River Spirit*, was shortlisted for the HWA Gold Crown Award for Historical Fiction. Aboulela grew up in Sudan. In her mid-twenties she moved to Scotland, where she now lives.

ALSO BY LEILA ABOULELA

LEILA ABOULELA

A New Year

A Quick Reads Original

SAQI

Chapter 1

When Suad's husband died, her three adult children came home. Her two sons arrived first. The youngest came by train and the eldest flew to London from Scotland. Suad's daughter travelled across the world from Indonesia. The children filled the house and surrounded her with love and support. They promised that they would look after her. They would never allow their mother to become lonely in her old age. Suad felt comforted and relieved. They were good Muslim children who would honour her forever. She was worried about being alone, but they would never throw her in a nursing home. They would not abandon her.

The death of Suad's husband, Sherif, had been a shock. In the morning, he showered, dressed and went to work. In the afternoon his body was in the morgue. He had been a maths teacher close to retirement. Sherif died in the staff room in the middle of lunch. When Sherif gasped and keeled over, the staff called an ambulance. It did not arrive quickly enough.

Suad's whole life had been turned upside down. Sherif had been her soulmate. He had been the one with the big plans but they talked through the details together. Suad kept Sherif grounded. He gave her the everyday strength to carry on.

Sherif had always been the one who explained things to Suad. He had dealt with all the difficulties – their immigration paperwork and how to live in a foreign country. They had moved to Britain to escape war. Now it was as if the horrors they had fled had reached her anyway. Suad was crushed and breathless. She swayed from the weight of the loss. Her man was gone. Suddenly. The end.

But no, Suad still had to break the news to their children. She called her eldest son first. Hamza was an engineer. He lived with his young family in the Scottish countryside. It did not completely surprise Hamza that his father would collapse. Sherif was seventy-three years old. He had been overweight, overworked, with high cholesterol, high blood pressure and a history of smoking. But death? Hamza was not expecting that.

Hamza had imagined they would rush to the hospital and spend days in intensive care. 'Yes, but it was not like that,' said Suad, starting to weep.

'Call Nesrine and Mazen,' Hamza said to Suad. 'I will get the next flight. I doubt Nesrine will be able to come.'

Nesrine, Suad's only daughter, lived in Jakarta with her husband. Two years ago, she had shocked her parents by insisting on marrying a divorced man twice her age. Suad knew how upsetting the call would be. It took a heartbeat for Nesrine to absorb the news. Then she became hysterical.

Crying bitterly, Nesrine insisted on coming home.

Suad's conversation with Mazen, the youngest, was the hardest. He was studying medicine in Birmingham and his father had been particularly proud of him. 'I don't understand what you're saying,' Mazen said. 'Where is Baba now right now? Is he at work or the hospital?'

Suad raised her voice. It was wobbly but loud. 'In the hospital. The school phoned me. They tried to save him. The school nurse did CPR until the ambulance came.'

'Okay. The hospital will know what to do,' Mazen said.

'No, Mazen. Your father's dead. Listen, come home. Go now to the train station and come home.'

'Mama, you should be with him. Get off the phone and talk to the doctors.'

It was a horrible conversation.

Mazen still refused to believe the news. His flatmates helped him catch the train to London. He was the first to arrive. Hamza flew from Inverness and landed at Heathrow airport after dark. Nesrine was the last to arrive. It took her almost thirty hours to reach home and she missed the funeral.

It was Muslim tradition to go ahead with the funeral as soon as possible. The funeral prayers were held in the mosque the day after Sherif's death. Mid-week, straight after the noon prayer. Understandably, not everyone could get away from work or studies. There was a decent number of people, but the prayer hall was not overflowing. Later, when Suad shared her disappointment with the children, they were horrified that she noticed. They did not understand why it mattered.

'You only have one funeral,' Suad said. One life. Death was huge. Death was final. Death was the experience everyone hated and everyone had to taste.

Suad wanted all of Sherif's students to be at his funeral prayers. She thought they should all have been at the mosque, paying their respects to their teacher and praying for his soul.

It was Suad's friends who filled the women's section of the mosque. Women she had known since she first moved to Britain forty years ago. They were all there. Every single one of them who was still alive. Many of these women could now only pray sitting on chairs. Some of them had survived awful illnesses. Some of them were already widowed.

Suad burst into tears when she saw the coffin. She could not hold herself up anymore. If her best friend Najla hadn't supported her, she would have fallen to the floor. Suad's body felt empty and dry. It was like being in the middle of storm.

Sherif's death was now real, Suad could not deny it. He was really going away. He did not belong to her anymore. He did not belong in his own home; he did not belong in the school where he taught. Even in the mosque where he had prayed, they were bidding him goodbye. When Suad cried, she felt helpless as if she were no longer a responsible adult. She struggled to see or hear.

When she was with Najla and her friends,

Suad gave way to grief. But with her children, she made a huge effort to stay calm and reasonable. The children must always come first, that's what Sherif had said. Everything Suad and Sherif had done had been for the children. It felt right that they were here now, with her. They had left studies and work. They had left partners and children.

It was painful not to be able to tell Sherif that the children came. There were so many things she wanted to ask him. Was it okay for Mazen to skip his lectures? Should she be the one phoning distant family or should Hamza, as the eldest son, do it? It felt crazy to think that Sherif could not answer. It was unfair that she was expected to continue alone.

Suad could not sleep. Sherif's smell was still on the sheets, but the bed was cold. She could not hear him breathing or snoring. It didn't make sense. It was all too quick. She phoned Najla. She had said call any time.

When Najla picked up, Suad said, 'I can't bear the pain. I am not well at all.'

Najla said, 'Pray for him, Suad. He needs you now. He can't pray. He can't do anything for himself. Ask Allah Almighty to forgive him. To wash away all his sins. To fill his grave with light. To grant him peace in that dark, lonely place where we are all heading.'

It comforted Suad to hear such words. Najla was right. Sherif had left against his will. He had gone and Suad would go there too one day, sooner or later. She must be patient. She would take comfort in her wonderful children. They were well brought up; they understood their duty towards her. They would look after her. They would not let her down.

Chapter 2

The day after the funeral, the children settled around their widowed mother. Hamza spoke to his work mates on the phone. Nesrine's friends came over. Suad glimpsed her youngest son, Mazen, in the garden talking to the neighbour across the fence. Everyone knew that Sherif was dead now.

Around the kitchen table, the children talked to each other while Suad heated up the food the neighbours had brought over. Suad was never going to heat up food for Sherif again. Never cook for him or take a mug of tea from him. There was a buzz in her ears, a pressure. She tried to stay calm for her children's sake but it was no good.

'I came with your father to this country and now he has left me,' she said and burst into tears. Sherif had sometimes talked of going back home. Suad had not believed this, but Sherif was keen. He had talked of being buried with his ancestors. Now, this dream was dashed forever. Suad would certainly not return on her own. Her future must be here.

Instead of eating with the children, she went to bed. The flat was split level. The bedrooms were in the basement and lead out to the garden. The kitchen and living room were on the ground floor, overlooking the street. Lying down, she could hear her children talking upstairs.

They were all exhausted and upset. Anything and everything could spark more tears. Suad and Mazen made the most noise when crying. Hamza was dry-eyed and Nesrine, after the initial hysterics, wept quietly.

It frustrated Suad that she could not ask Sherif his opinion. Would he have wanted her to do this or that? It hurt her head. Simple things confused her. She had forgotten to take her medication, but how many times? She needed to get back to everyone who had sent her messages. She would start to listen to her voicemails but then lose concentration. She tried to remember the last thing Sherif had said to her. It had been such an ordinary day. The evening before was ordinary too.

The next day when Suad woke up her head was clearer. There were practical matters to resolve. Paperwork. Insurance. The death certificate.

Strangely, Suad found herself competent, alert, able to deal with all these things. Thinking about them was a distraction from feeling her pain. Sherif's car had been left at the school. It needed to be brought home. Where were his car keys? Where were all the things Sherif had with him – a Tupperware box with his lunch, his phone, his wallet? Had he died before finishing his lunch?

Three days passed, then five days, then a week, and the family began to settle. When one of them cried now, it was because of something new they saw. Nesrine came across photos of herself as a little girl in her father's arms. Photos taken in playgrounds and the zoo. Tears ran down Hamza's face when he collected his father's car, the same one Sherif had taught Hamza to drive in. Mazen cried when he used his father's phone charger because he had lost his own. Suad washed Sherif's clothes that were still in the laundry basket. The shirts, underwear and pyjamas smelled strongly of him.

The manner of Sherif's death troubled Suad. Suddenly, in the staff room. Sherif could have died in many other ways. Better ways. He could have died in his sleep, peacefully, right next to her, safe in their bed. He could have died in hospital, like most people do, after friends and the children had visited him to say goodbye. In hospital, Sherif would have appreciated the medical care he was getting. He would have compared his good surroundings to the dismal conditions people like him faced back home. He would have made these comparisons and he would have been grateful.

Even better than a hospital, Sherif could have died at the mosque, in the middle of prayers. This would have been a death to be proud of. This would have been proof that he was a good religious man, with his heart in the right place. Instead, he had died at work as if work was the most important part of his life. Sherif had been a good teacher but teaching maths had never been his dream job.

Sherif had trained as an architect before he came to Britain. For a long time, he said he was an architect even though he did not have the correct qualifications to work as one in Britain. Instead, he signed up for a local authorities' scheme to train maths teachers. He was an ideal candidate. He did well and spent a lifetime teaching. Still, Suad did not believe that he had been passionate enough about his job to die at work.

The children went over the last time they were back and forth with their father on

WhatsApp. Hamza had posted a photo of his wife, Zahra, celebrating her fortieth birthday on the family group chat. 'Happy Birthday Zahra', they had all written, with emojis of birthday cakes, balloons and hearts. Sherif had written, 'Happy Birthday, Zayra. May all your days be happy. May our family always be blessed.' He had misspelt Zahra's name and no one had corrected him.

Then, only ten days after Sherif's death, Suad heard Nesrine loudly crying and laughing in her room. She was talking to her husband in Jakarta. Nesrine came out into the corridor and thrust her phone in front of Suad. It took Suad a few moments to understand what she was looking at. It looked like a photo of a Covid test. Nesrine giggled. No, it was a positive pregnancy test!

The weight of the good news was unbearable to Suad. She had known that Nesrine had been trying for a baby, but it did not feel right to celebrate. Nesrine's face was flushed with happiness. It took all of Suad's willpower not to push her away. 'Congratulations, congratulations,' she whispered. 'Your father would have been so happy.'

Nesrine hugged her mother, but Suad untangled herself. She rushed to the bathroom and locked the door. She breathed in and out. This was how mourning was. It was moving in sorrow. It was finding darkness normal. It was finding laughter and song all wrong. Sunshine and bright colours unnatural. Inside her daughter's stomach a new life pulsed. It felt too soon, too soon. Suad could not celebrate. She was not ready yet.

Fortunately, Nesrine did not want to announce the news of her pregnancy publicly. Suad was spared congratulations from her close friends and family. Phone calls in which she would have had to sound happy and grateful. Conversations in which it was appropriate to marvel on how God takes and gives. How small and insignificant Nesrine's baby was compared to Sherif's long, full life! He had worked so hard. He had given a sound education to many engineers, computer programmers, auditors and certified accountants in the community.

Tears poured down Suad's face. She would have liked a few more leisurely years for her husband. She would have liked for him to retire, so he could spend time in the mosque and meeting his friends in the local coffee shop. The two of them had only recently started to enjoy the privacy of their empty nest and to feel like a couple again.

Suad was a retired nurse. She had wanted to nurse Sherif in his last illness and pray with him on his deathbed. But this had not happened. This was Fate, this was Destiny, this was Allah's will and Suad must accept it.

Chapter 3

Hamza was the first to leave London. He needed to get back to the office. He also felt uncomfortable leaving his wife, Zahra, and their two children by themselves for so long. Their house was deep in the Scottish countryside. The nearest neighbour was far away.

Mazen, in a fit of temper, announced that he had missed lab work and too many classes. 'They will make me repeat the year and I would rather drop out,' he announced. Suad was alarmed. She couldn't believe it. He had only been at home for two weeks! He stormed off to the train station. Nesrine comforted her mother. 'Mazen has always been a drama queen. He is not serious about dropping out.'

Nesrine was at home for the longest time because she had come the furthest distance. She stayed for three weeks, then she announced that she was going to fly back to Jakarta the following week. Suad dreaded her daughter's departure. She had never lived alone. She could not imagine it. Nesrine's presence in the house soothed her. Even when Nesrine didn't sit with her, even when she kept to her room or went out on her own, Suad felt comforted.

Nesrine was suffering from morning sickness. It reminded Suad of her own pregnancies and she began to look forward to the baby. She had a wealth of experience and enjoyed sharing it with her daughter. 'You must follow custom,' she said to Nesrine. 'If the baby is a boy, you must name him after your father.'

Suad was disappointed by Nesrine's cool reply. Nesrine said that she and her husband were considering many names. Suad wanted to tell Sherif this. He always listened with sympathy to her worries – about the children and everything else. The wide space he had left could never be filled.

When Nesrine finally returned to Jakarta, the flat felt big and silent. There was no need to put on a brave face. Najla, who had been visiting regularly, was away on holiday with her family. There was little reason to get out of bed in the morning or change her clothes. There was no need for Suad to cook now. When Najla phoned to check up on Suad, Suad lied and said she was eating properly.

Tuesday was exactly like Wednesday. What

was the difference? Even Sunday was like Monday. For so many years, Monday had been the start of the week. An important day, when Sherif went to work and Suad volunteered at the mosque. Now all the days were the same.

Hours of memories. A marriage of forty-six years. Suad's mind swept back and forth. She could remember the very early years, back home, before the war. The wedding drums. Her grandmother had been alive then, and so had Sherif's father and his brother who they lost in the war. Sometimes Suad's memories were like missing photos, sometimes they were of things said and felt. She remembered a day, near the beginning of the war, when Sherif went out and didn't come home for hours. There were no mobile phones then. She had rocked baby Hamza in her arms and waited anxiously by the window, looking out at the bombed street. When Sherif came back, he was sweaty and scared. He had been delayed by the army's new check points.

Suad remembered the first time she had met Sherif. It had been at his cousin's wedding. 'Why aren't you eating?' he had said to her. He was carrying a huge platter of spinach fatayer. 'Eat. Eat.' He had urged her to have a second and a third helping. His insistence had made her giggle. She had not known that the bride, her best friend from college, had such an attractive cousin. 'Sherif is a catch,' Suad's mother later said to her. 'Lucky girl.'

The happy memories brought tears to her eyes. Hot, gentle tears. The clearer the memory, the more satisfied Suad was. She did not need photo albums. Besides, searching for photos felt like a chore. Suad could not sort out Sherif's drawers. She had tried to offer some of his things to the children. But instead of being pleased with their father's watch, a sweater he had never worn and his new briefcase, the children turned them down. They thought their father's things were old-fashioned.

Hamza called more regularly than his siblings. He was the eldest and the most responsible. Two months after Sherif's death, he was more worried about Suad than ever. 'I don't like how you're sounding,' he said. 'Zahra will come and stay with you.'

Suad objected. She did not want her daughter-in-law to stay. She liked Zahra, but the house was in no state for guests! Still, Hamza insisted. Suad tried to prepare. She must clean the house. She must cook a welcome meal. She must get showered and dressed. It was too much. She had no energy. After a half-hearted attempt, she crawled back into bed. She waited, her heart beating, for the doorbell to ring.

'I don't need you here,' Suad snapped at Zahra when she arrived. 'Go back to your husband and children.' Suad was embarrased. Would Zahra spend the rest of her life recounting how she had heroically saved her mother-in-law? Suad knew she was in a terrible slump. At the very least, Zahra said she was dehydrated. Zahra went shopping for groceries and made soup for Suad. She fed her like a child. She cajoled her into the shower. She helped her into a fresh new nightie. She changed the bedsheets and put the washing machine on. Suad heard Zahra on the phone to Hamza that night. Suad was bitter. Was Zahra boasting about all her achievements? Was she telling Hamza how useless his mother was? Suad did not like watching Zahra move around *her* kitchen, using *her* things.

However, soon Suad did start to feel better. Zahra made sure that her mother-in-law was eating proper meals and drinking enough water. Zahra went to the pharmacy and came back with laxatives and sleeping pills. They both worked like magic. Now Suad was sleeping more soundly and her stomach was a lot better.

Zahra treated Suad like she was unwell, which was exactly what Suad needed. She was sick. Sick with sorrow. She was exhausted. She needed her bed. She could not face the world. It had all been too much. Too much shock. Too many phone calls. Too many house guests staying for too long. She felt guilty about being mean to Zahra.

'I will not leave you until you are well and strong!' Zahra promised. She was indeed an angel.

As a sign of progress, she managed to get Suad out of bed and onto the living room couch with a blanket wrapped around her legs. Zahra put the television on. Suad found nature programmes soothing. She would turn down the sound and just look at the greenery and jungles. Mothers feeding their infants. A litter of African lion cubs. A nest of chicks.

Back where Suad was born, widows in mourning did not watch television. They did not eat sweets. All this Suad explained to Zahra. Zahra was a good listener. She was interested in these old traditions. Her parents were immigrants too.

Suad grew more fond of Zahra. She found her easy to talk to. 'You are closer to me than Nesrine, my own flesh and blood,' she said. But Zahra had already stayed for a whole week and Suad knew that she couldn't stay forever. It was a shame Scotland was so far away from London.

Chapter 4

'I want you to come with me to Scotland,' Zahra said. Suad was much better, and Zahra was ready to head back home to Hamza and the children.

'You belong with us. You belong with your eldest son and his family,' Zahra said.

'I will think about it,' Suad said. 'But first I must help Mazen. He must pass his exams.'

In every phone call, Mazen threatened to drop out of university. Sherif would be appalled if Mazen did not finish his degree. He had been so proud that his youngest child would become a doctor. Ever since his dad died, Mazen had been sleeping in and missing the practical part of his clinical training. He was unable to complete ward rounds. In the lab, he got all the specimens wrong.

Suad felt a sense of responsibility towards Mazen. He needed her now and she must go to him. Sherif would have wanted her to do this. She must push herself. She could do it.

21

It was easy to lock the door and leave. Home without Sherif was not home. Once Zahra caught the train back to Scotland, the flat felt too big and empty again. There were echoes and shadows. Without Sherif's warmth, the walls around Suad were damp and tight. She started noticing that she was down, under the street, far away from other people. It made her uncomfortable and she was relieved to get away.

It took a few hours by train to get to the town where Mazen studied. Suad propped her suitcase on the luggage rack and found a seat. It felt strange to be out of the house, among strangers. Everything seemed too loud and bright. People were hurrying and jostling. They were munching crisps and texting. Suad sat huddled in the corner of the train carriage. She felt nervous but determined. Mazen didn't know that she was coming to stay with him.

Mazen shared a flat with two other students. He was shocked to find his mother at the door. 'Who do you think you are?' he said. 'Mary Poppins?'

Suad was coming to steady her son. She thought she could prevent him from abandoning his dream of becoming a doctor. Mazen looked terrible. Thin and wretched, with a wild look in his eyes. There was a stale smell in his room, used cutlery on the floor and piles of clothes that could or could not be dirty laundry.

Mazen did not hide the fact that his mother was not welcome. 'You're not staying? Seriously? How long? Where are you going to sleep?'

There was only one bed in his room. 'I will sleep on the floor,' she said.

Mazen groaned. 'Please Mama. Please go back home. I beg you.'

'I won't leave until you are studying again.' She bustled around the room, tidying up. She unpacked her few belongings. She had not forgotten all the necessary spices – cardamom, mint, coriander. Everything she needed to cook decent meals.

'You will pull your socks up and become a doctor. You will not fail. I will not let you.'

'This is a nightmare. What am I going to tell my flatmates?'

'You will tell them the truth,' she said, opening the window. A gust of fresh air came in.

Mazen grumbled for a whole day before accepting Suad's prescence. The following morning, mother and son formulated a plan of action. It shocked Suad that Mazen had not informed his lecturers that Sherif had died. 'You must ask for help', she insisted. 'All your teachers must know your circumstances. It has only been three months since your dad passed away.'

Suad encouraged Mazen to make an appointment with the Students' Counselling Services. She applauded his decision to start Bereavement Therapy. She made sure he woke up on time in the morning. She made him coffee and got him out the door. During the day, she cooked his favourite meals and tidied his desk. He settled into a work routine, grudgingly at first, but then more willingly.

'I'm doing this to get rid of you,' he said. He was only half joking.

She agreed with him and promised to leave as soon as he was back on track.

'I am going to the library to escape from you,' he said.

'Go with my blessing.'

When he came back from the library, Suad would look at Mazen closely. She was able to tell whether he had been studying or spending the time dawdling and brooding. There was a special look in his eyes when he had been concentrating. Sherif had had that same look when he was working on study plans or marking tests.

The whole flat needed cleaning, not just Mazen's room. The kitchen was a disaster zone.

The bathroom took hours of scrubbing. It took Suad several days of hard work before she was satisfied that the flat was liveable. All the energy flooding through her body surprised her. It felt good to be of use. To help Mazen. To save him from throwing his future away.

She now cooked for all the flatmates, not only her son. It seemed silly not to do so. They appreciated her food and polished off every morsel. Cooking gave way to washing the dishes. Suad took over the kitchen. She cleaned the fridge, which looked like it had never been cleaned in its life. She dusted and vacuumed the whole flat. It was tiring staying with Mazen, but worthwhile. However, sleeping on the floor was hurting her back.

Nesrine was outraged when Suad told her what she was doing. On video calls from Jakarta, she shouted at her mother. 'No one does that. No one cooks and cleans for strangers. No one sleeps on their floor overnight? This is ridiculous. Mama, you are being exploited.'

Suad laughed. 'I am fine, don't worry about me. Mazen needs me.'

'I need you too,' Nesrine shrieked. 'I am the one going through a difficult pregnancy. I want you to come and stay with me. I will send you the flight tickets.'

Suad asked Nesrine for a little bit more time. She still did not feel comfortable leaving Mazen. Also, it was months before the baby's arrival and the doctors were satisfied with Nesrine's condition.

When the weather improved, Suad went out for walks. The streets did not have a past which included Sherif. It felt so unnatural to be without him, but she spoke to him in her mind. She commented on things she was seeing that would have interested him.

On one occasion, she was stopped by a young lady with a tablet device. Did Suad have a few minutes to spare? Would she participate in a survey about the future of the city centre? Yes, Suad would be happy to do so.

There were the usual questions. Age, ethnicity. What was her marital status?

Suad was married of course, married for over forty years, married for longer than the life of the young lady who was asking the question. But no, wait! Suad was not married anymore. She was widowed. She was half of what she had always been. She had lost the job of 'wife', the role, the position. Sherif had been her home and now she was a wanderer, without a home.

Even Mazen noticed his mother's sad mood that evening. Suad did not ask him about his work. She did not, as she usually did, pray in a loud voice for his success. These prayers – that the exams would be easy and that he would find success – always filled Mazen with comfort and confidence. Tonight, Suad was withdrawn.

Mazen opened his laptop and started to show Suad images of the human heart. For the first time, he spoke about his father's death. He spoke about it from a medical point of view. A sudden cardiac arrest not a heart attack. He explained the difference to her. He spoke in a clear, kind voice. Informed, practical and calm. He spoke like a doctor.

'Our son is a doctor, Sherif. I wish you were here. I wish you were here to see his success.' Suad whispered under her breath.

She slept better that night. When she opened her eyes in the morning, Mazen was already dressed and ready to go to his hospital placement. He looked bright and eager.

It was time for Suad to move on. She had stayed with Mazen for a whole month. Today she would pack and leave. Nesrine wanted her to help get everything ready for the baby. She had even booked Suad's flight to Jakarta. Suad must go back to London and prepare for the trip.

'I'm sure you're relieved to see the back of

me,' she said to Mazen, when he hugged her goodbye.

Chapter 5

This was Suad's first visit to Jakarta. It was the first time that she had travelled such a long distance by plane. Suad and Sherif had often talked of making this journey together. Now, she was doing it alone. Outside the airport, the temperature was warm and humid. It smelt of rain.

Nesrine and her husband, Mo, were waiting by the crowded terminal for Suad. Suad and Sherif had never approved of Mo. He did not have a university degree and he worked in hospitality. He was also burdened with an ex-wife and teenage children. He was not what they were looking for in a son-in-law, but Nesrine had insisted.

'There are so many sights to show you in Jakarta,' said Mo, helping Suad with her suitcase. She had not known what to pack. She was planning to stay for four whole months, until her grandchild arrived.

Mo wore a colourful shirt and played loud

dance music in the car. 'We will take you to Bali for a weekend,' he raised his voice so that she could hear him above the music.

'I am in mourning,' Suad replied. 'I am not here for fun and sightseeing.'

Mo and Nesrine exchanged looks.

Mo was the manager of a four-stars hotel in the city centre. To Suad's surprise, Mo and Nesrine lived in the hotel. They had a suite on the top floor. All this was introduced by Nesrine as glamorous and wonderful. She had talked non-stop during the long, slow-moving ride from the airport. Pregnancy suited her. She looked healthy and fulfilled.

The hotel suite had two bedrooms. Suad's room was going to be the baby's room. There was already a crib and a stack of unopened packages. She must squeeze in.

From the moment she arrived, life in a hotel suite felt strange to Suad. The constant, irritating ping of the lift in the corridor. The air conditioner carried smells she could not identify. None of the windows opened. Through floor to ceiling glass panes, the city sprawled down below her. She could see opulent villas with blue squares of swimming pools. She could see brown cardboard slums, with their crowded conditions and sluggish movements.

Suad did her best to keep her opinions to herself. She could tell that Nesrine and Mo were trying to make her feel welcome. They were kind and considerate. Mo took her to the city's biggest mosque. Suad was impressed and happy to be in the world's most populated Muslim country. How well the Qur'an was recited, by people for whom Arabic was not their mother tongue!

Nesrine took Suad shopping to buy lighter clothes suitable for the heat. The traffic was horrendous. The malls were crowded. Only Extra Large outfits fitted Suad. 'You are not fat, Mama,' Nesrine said, eager to reassure her. 'Asian sizes are a smaller fit than British ones.' Suad liked her new clothes – loose cotton trousers with a tunic and a matching scarf. They were sensible, inexpensive and kept her cool.

After three months, Suad got used to Jakarta. She did not feel at home, but she was beginning to grasp the routine, or at least, the lack of it.

Mo popped in and out all the time – he did not work regular hours. Or, according to him, he was always working. It rattled Suad that she could not predict his comings and goings. His naps and bathroom breaks. Suad wished Sherif was here. They would have fumed together. She called Najla to complain instead.

Worst of all was the food! Nesrine and Mo ordered room service constantly. Indonesian food was alien to Suad. Snacks wrapped up in banana leaves. Rice for breakfast. Hardly any bread or cheese or yoghurt. The suite did have a kitchen, but it was poorly equipped and hardly used. Waiters came in with the food, pushing trolleys. Everyday a different set of hotel staff cleaned the rooms. They were all polite and friendly, but it was a baffling lifestyle. Surely it was not the right environment to bring up a child?

Suad spent most of her time each day sitting in a lounge chair by the hotel pool in the shade. Nesrine would often join her in the afternoons, when they would sip iced tea together (a new taste Suad had acquired). She enjoyed looking at the children swimming with their colourful floats. Next to her Nesrine sat scrolling through her tablet. She had abandoned her hijab after meeting Mo. With time, her clothes were becoming skimpier. The dresses shorter, the cleavage deeper. It did not help that her stomach and breasts were expanding.

One day they were waiting for their drinks to arrive when Mo soon appeared, not to Suad's great surprise. That man was always hovering. He shared a few words with the lifeguard and then joined Nesrine to look closely at the tablet. More shopping for the baby, no doubt.

Suad overheard them deliberate car seats. 'You are buying too much,' she said. 'Babies don't need so many things.'

'I want my daughter to have the best of everything,' Nesrine said. 'I want her to be better than me.'

'You and your brothers had everything you needed and more,' Suad said, turning to take a glass of iced tea from the waiter.

Nesrine snorted. 'We lived in poverty.'

'Poverty!' Suad watched the waiter leave before responding to her daughter. 'What do you know about poverty? Your father worked all hours. I worked nightshifts! I broke my back working.' She had raised her voice without realising it. The lifeguard glanced towards them. Suad went on. She was upset. 'You had new shoes, food on the table, Eid gifts! You had your own room, Nesrine. Your father paid in full for the heating. He took you to the zoo, everything you asked for!'

'That's not true,' Nesrine said quietly. 'We never went on holiday. Not a single holiday. I wasn't allowed sleepovers with friends or to go to concerts. I wasn't allowed Christmas presents. I begged for a puppy, but it was no.

He said no to everything.'

'Nonsense!' said Suad. She could not bear to hear any criticism of Sherif. 'Your father loved you. And you were proud of him being the maths teacher at school.'

'Proud?' Nesrine scoffed. 'The children made fun of him. All the time! They would mimic his accent. *Young–est–ters.* He couldn't even say "youngsters". He said young–est–ters.'

'Stop it,' Suad said, hurt. She couldn't understand where this argument had come from. They had been having a nice day. She suddenly felt very hot. 'You're ungrateful and disrespectful!'

'Lower your voices!' Said Mo. Suad had forgotten he was behind her. 'We are in a public place!'

This angered Suad even more. She pullled herself up straight and jabbed her finger at Mo. 'And why are we in a public place? Because *you* can't provide your wife with her own home! Why can't you live at home and go to work each day like all men do? Is a hotel full of all sorts of strangers the right place to bring up a child?'

Mo looked stern. 'This is a private matter between me and Nesrine,' he said.

Nesrine suddenly stood up with a heave.

Suad thought she had spilled her drink. But the stain on Nesrine's dress and the puddle on the floor were something else. 'My waters!' gasped Nesrine, clutching her stomach and staring at the floor.

It was a long labour. Suad and Mo became a team helping Nesrine. The earlier argument was forgotten or at least pushed aside. Suad felt sympathy for Nesrine. She felt her labour pains as if they were her own. That was an exaggeration of course, but Suad's body was also somehow involved. Physical memories rushed back and Suad once again had the awesome feel of a newborn baby in her arms.

It was touching how much Nesrine clung to her, how much she needed her mother's advice and guidance. Mo was supportive but this was not his first child. His was not the kind of job which granted paternity leave. Suad was the one who stayed with Nesrine overnight at the hospital.

Suad whispered prayers in the baby's ears. A tiny little girl who looked like her mother. Nesrine could now understand motherhood. 'See how much pain I went through to bring you into the world,' Suad told her. 'Now you know!'

The first minutes of the baby's life, the

first night. The baby learning how to feed. Nesrine's milk coming in. The doctor satisfied with mum and baby. Getting discharged from hospital. Arriving home for the first time to a warm welcome from the hotel staff. Suad was part of all this and it brought her satisfaction. She needed to feel helpful. To be useful to the children like she had been useful to Sherif. To have an important role in the family. It was bliss to just sit with the baby in her arms while Nesrine had a shower.

A week after the birth Suad fell ill with food poisoning. It was as if every drop of fluid in her body wanted to get out. Back and forth between bed and the bathroom. Spasms of pain. She was mortified by the ugliness of her condition. This was the baby's room. It should be pure and beautiful. What a nuisance Suad had become! How awkward to be an ill guest!

The hotel doctor came to see her. He sent her to hospital. She felt wretched, surrounded by nurses who, although kind and efficient, could not speak English. She was prescribed pills and sachets to drink and nagged to be discharged. Despite being busy with the baby, and the argument by the pool, Nesrine and Mo were kind and caring. Mo even brought pitta bread from a special bakery. It was the kind of bread

Suad was used to, which was not available in the local supermarket. Suad was grateful for the bread. She ate it with honey to keep up her strength.

Suad recovered but continued to feel weak. Her illness made her impatient. The weather, the food and life in the hotel – all felt alien and annoying. Even her damp, lonely, underground flat in London was better than this! Suad vowed not to stay a day longer than the baby's six-week birthday. Besides, Hamza and Zahra were urging her to stay with them in Scotland. Suad hadn't seen Hamza and Zahra's children since Sherif died. She missed them. Hamza booked her a flight to Edinburgh.

Suad began to count the days until her travel to Scotland. A month to go, half-way through, ten days left. The baby was opening her eyes more, sleeping less. She filled the clothes that were newborn size. Every morning, after the dawn prayers, Suad looked after the baby so that Nesrine could sleep in. Gradually, Nesrine became more active. She pushed the pram down the hotel corridors and out to the pool. Three days to go. Two more days to go.

It was agreed that Suad would go to the airport on the hotel shuttle. Nesrine walked with her to the door of the suite. The porter was there to take her luggage downstairs. Suad kissed Nesrine goodbye then decided to visit the toilet one last time before leaving. All the travel nerves had affected her bladder!

As she opened the door to go back inside, Suad heard Mo crooning to the baby, 'ding dong, the witch is gone!' The words did not make sense to Suad. It must have been an inappropriate song because Nesrine, hugging her goodbye again, looked very embarrassed.

Chapter 6

Suad was pleased that she was going to Scotland. She felt it was right for her to be with Hamza and his family. It was proper that her eldest son should be responsible for her. He was the most settled of the three children, not the one who needed her the most. And Zahra was the best daughter-in-law a woman could hope for. She welcomed Suad with open arms. The house was tidy and prepared. The children displayed their best manners and there was a lovely meal on the table.

This house in the Scottish countryside was familiar to Suad and she was fond of it. It held memories of Sherif. They had visited together many times over the years. The cupboards in the guest room, where she was now staying by herself, still had some of her warm cardigans, dresses and socks from their last trip here. The umbrella she had bought last winter was still hanging on the peg by the front door.

There were also traces of her husband. A pair

of rubber slippers he had used for the bathroom. A copy of the Qur'an with the ribbon bookmark marking the last page he had read. Suad could feel him all around her. The memories and a sense of his approval.

They had enjoyed coming here for a break in their city lives. They had been satisfied that Hamza was doing well in his career and marriage. They had enjoyed their grandchildren – Yousef, who wore glasses and resembled his mother and Maha who was chubby and a mirror image of her aunt Nesrine at the same age.

The children became emotional when they came home from school and saw Suad alone. Here was the proof that their grandfather was gone and never coming back. Suad hugged them but she didn't cry.

'I'm sad about Grandpa,' Maha said.

'Me too,' said Suad. She was relieved to be with them. Here she was on stable ground. She felt at home with them.

She showed her grandchildren a photo of Nesrine's newborn baby, the cousin who, unlike them, would never meet her grandfather. She told them stories of her time in Jakarta. The beautiful birds she had seen, the banana trees and the day a mongoose scampered on the roof of the hotel and frightened the guests. Now that she was no longer there, Indonesia was an adventure rather than a place she had disliked.

Hamza and Zahra's house was spacious, with an open-plan kitchen and a dining area. The kitchen had a breakfast island surrounded by stools. The sitting room was all done up in calm, beige tones. The house was set back from the main road. It was far from the neighbouring houses. From the window of her room, Suad could see acres and acres of heather. She could see cows in the farms across the road. The autumn colours of Scotland mirrored her mood, complimented her sadness. These watery colours showed her that loss and pain could have beauty and a dignity too.

The nearest town was a thirty-minute drive away. The children went to school on a bus, even though Hamza and Zahra each had a car. Hamza worked long hours and sometimes had to travel on business trips. Zahra, who was an accountant in the housing department of the local council, worked flexible hours. Twice a week she worked from home. On these days, she did the housework and the cooking, moving back and forth between the dining table and the kitchen.

After a fortnight or so, when she had got into the routine, Suad offered to help around the house. But Zahra would say, 'rest Auntie, you've been through so much.' Suad did rest. The weather was cold and blustery; going out for walks was not appealing. Suad watched television and spent a long time on the telephone. She caught up with all the people who had reached out to her after Sherif's death. She spoke to Najla every week. Nesrine video-called and shared how the baby was growing. The mornings passed, then Suad would change and wait for the children to come home from school.

She wanted to greet them with a snack, but Zahra was anxious about Maha's weight and restricted her sugar intake. 'It's just her age,' Suad said. 'Both Nesrine and I had a chubby phase and then we got over it.' Zahra, who had been thin all her life, was not reassured by Suad's words.

On the other hand, Zahra was very relaxed about Yousef's weakness in maths. He was in the bottom group of his class and both Zahra and Hamza were okay with that. 'He is strong in English and Arts,' they said.

'But his grandfather was a maths teacher!' Suad complained. Sherif had noted Yousef's struggles from an early age and coached him in the holidays. Now, the boy was left to struggle with his maths homework on his own. Suad offered to help, but Zahra didn't seem keen, preferring to supervise her children's homework herself.

The weekends were best. On Saturday mornings, Zahra caught up with the household chores while Suad, Hamza and the children went into town. The children went to swimming lessons. Hamza and Suad had a coffee in a delightful café. This always felt like a treat and Suad enjoyed Hamza's company. He was the one she could talk to most about Sherif, the life they had left behind and their early days in Britain.

On Sundays, Suad was allowed (it felt like that) to cook for the family. They liked her crunchy falafel, which she enjoyed making from scratch. She used an ice cream scoop to shape the balls, tossing them in the hot oil one after the other. Everyone agreed that they were vastly superior to any takeout.

A month after Suad had arrived in Scotland, Mazen came to Hamza's house to stay for the Christmas holidays. It felt special to Suad to have her two sons with her. Mazen shared the guest room with her and late at night, when everyone else went to bed, Suad spoke to him about Hamza and his family.

'I don't understand why they live so far away from everything,' she whispered. 'The children are missing out on visits to friends and after-school activities.'

'That's not fair, Mama. Hamza takes them swimming. And they see their friends after school.'

'It's not the same though,' she murmured. 'I think they should move.'

Mazen sat up. 'Don't start interfering! Is it true you rearranged the kitchen cupboards?'

Suad shrugged. 'Everything was in the wrong place. What was I meant to do!'

Mazen groaned, 'Please don't mess up. You're happy and I'm able to focus better on my studies knowing you're here and not on your own.'

'I'm not settled,' she hissed. 'My flat, your father's flat – I've just abandoned it. I don't like that. We need to decide about it. I wanted us to be there now. We could have got it sorted. I suggested to Hamza that we all go to London for the holidays. Hamza said yes, it was a good idea.'

'To be honest, that would have been more convenient for me,' said Mazen, lying down again. 'Instead of coming all the way up here. And now tomorrow I have the long journey back.'

'Zahra stopped it,' Suad whispered. 'I wanted to be the one hosting you all. One last time. But she wanted it to be her house, her kitchen, her best dishes.'

'Give her a break,' said Mazen. 'She's working hard to make you feel welcome.'

'It's all about duty for her,' said Suad. 'I don't think she even likes me.'

'Then get her to like you,' said Mazen. 'She cooked a great meal today and you didn't say one nice thing about it. Not a single compliment!'

Suad sniffed. 'The fuss she made getting hold of a halal turkey. Why should we eat turkey anyway! Your father hated it. He said it was too dry.'

She could hear by Mazen's breathing that he was falling asleep. A wave of loneliness hit her. But no, not now, not today. Today had been good. Nesrine had video-called earlier on, the startled baby thrust in front of the camera. Yousef and Maha were thrilled to see their baby cousin. It had all been warm and fun. Suad should be grateful. She was grateful. So why this sudden loneliness? Mazen was snoring now. In his twenties and he was snoring! She couldn't remember him snoring when she stayed with him. It must be Zahra's rich cooking and that rubbery bird.

Unsettled, Suad went out to the sitting room. Zahra, a model of efficiency, had tidied everything away. The dining table was cleared and the dishwater was humming. Suad parted the curtains and peered out into the night. There was snow as far as the eye could see. A thick white sheet covering the dead ground like a shroud. Spring and rebirth, fresh green and new growth, were still to come.

Chapter 7

Suad took up online shopping. It was the Boxing Day sales that got her started. Miraculously, things got delivered in the middle of nowhere. This proved to be a great source of excitement. Choosing what she wanted, putting the order through, anticipating its arrival. When January came around and Zahra went back to work, Suad managed to schedule delivery dates. She did not want parcels arriving when Zahra was working from home. She did not want the sound of the doorbell to disturb her. She did not want Zahra to ask, 'what did you order, Auntie? Show me.' Then after showing her, Zahra would likely say something like, 'oh, we have this already.' 'Oh, I could have got it for you much cheaper.' 'Oh, why on earth do you need this!'

The three days of the week when Zahra went to the office were Suad's days of freedom. She could do what she liked. The first thing she did was turn off the heating, which was a terrible extravagance. Freedom sometimes meant having a good loud cry. Freedom was also wandering around in her nightdress, banging around in the kitchen, having the television on full blast. It also meant anticipating the deliveries. An electric blanket. Toiletries. A tray so that she could eat in front of the television. Bars of chocolate.

The chocolates were the greatest secret. They had to reach her room undetected by Zahra or Hamza. Even Yousef was not entirely to be trusted. He could be a snitch. The chocolates were mainly for Maha. The poor girl was denied all sweets and Suad felt so sorry for her. It was such a pleasure to have Maha in the room where, breathlessly, they could share a bar of chocolate together. Maha's eyes would light up. She would savour every bite. Half a bar for each school day or a lollipop or a bag of jellybeans. Surely that was okay. Suad had brought up children before. They were never denied sweets. Zahra was being unreasonable.

Another purchase hidden from Zahra was an old-fashioned abacus for teaching maths. The beads were red and white. On the evenings when Zahra was not yet back from the office, Suad would take out the abacus and practise maths with Yousef. It was an excellent learning tool. Suad was convinced that Yousef was progressing. She didn't forbid him from telling his parents. However, she never mentioned the abacus in their presence, nor did she bring it out on the days Zahra was working from home. When Yousef surprised his parents by doing well in his latest maths assignment, Suad kept her mouth shut. She winked at Yousef across the dining table.

Once a fortnight, the children came to her room for a sleepover. They would bring their sleeping bags and settle around her, excited by the change in routine. She loved praying with their limbs so close to her. She enjoyed telling them spooky stories and watching the lights in their eyes. She told them about her childhood, how she used to swim in a warm, salty sea. Some waves were small and gentle while others were as huge as houses. A favourite activity was showing them old photos that she had scanned on her phone. Photos of her wedding long go. Photos of their father as a baby. Here was Sherif with their aunt Nesrine and here Suad was in her nurse uniform. Yes, she had been a nurse. Then she had jarred her neck and back moving a faulty bed. That was why she had retired early. The children were impressed.

Whenever Zahra went into town, she asked Suad to accompany her. This usually happened on days that she was not working or times when Hamza was away. Suad always welcomed these outings. She had been so independent in London, popping out to the corner shop, hopping on buses, diving into the underground. Now, she could not go anywhere without a car. There was a local bus and it had a timetable. But it was a good quarter of an hour walk to the bus stop in the bitter Scottish winter. This did not appeal to Suad.

A day out with Zahra was hectic. Short on time, Zahra dashed around completing one errand after another. There was no time to browse shops. Suad always ended up feeling dissatisfied.

The leisurely coffee shop outings were on Saturdays with Hamza. Here she could share her anxiety about the flat in London. She had left it in a rush when she first went to Mazen and then flew to Nesrine. Now she was here and she had still not sorted out Sherif's things.

'It's been ten months, almost a year. We can't leave it like that,' she said.

'Someone needs to help you clear it up. Give away things. Sell them. It's full of junk.'

Suad didn't like the word 'junk'. Her house, her memories. The coffee came with a little macaroon, wrapped in paper. Suad put it in her handbag. A treat for Maha.

'It can only be you,' she said. 'Mazen is too busy.'

'But I'll need to take time off work,' said Hamza. 'It's a big ask.'

Suad suppressed a sharp reply. She did not like the note of boredom in Hamza's voice. Already his father was in the past. Hamza's life was here, his work, his children. His wife who kept him on his toes.

When they finished their coffees, he said, 'I might take longer picking up the children from swimming because I want to speak to the instructor. Just wait for me here and I'll send you a text when we're outside.'

Suad watched him leave. Every table around her was full and there were more people coming in. She put on her coat and went outside. Next door there was an estate agent. She looked at the photos that were on display at the window. There were houses within walking distance of where she was now. Smaller, certainly, but much more conveniently situated. Why couldn't Hamza and Zahra live in a house like that! Could they not afford it, if they sold theirs? It would certainly enhance the children's lives to be in town.

Suad entered the estate agency to look at

more photos. It was warm and pleasant inside. An assistant came to speak to her. 'Are you interested in the new retirement village?' she asked. She was a tall, pretty girl with wavy red hair. She gestured towards a display, a model of apartments, bungalows and cottages. She started to talk about the fitness studio, coffee lounge and hobby room. She explained the difference between independent and assisted living.

Suad listened to every word. It all sounded unreal, something strange to share with Najla on the phone. Suad had never lived alone. Ever, in her whole life. She had grown up in a busy household of siblings and elderly grandparents. When she first married Sherif, they had lived with his family, his unmarried younger sisters and an ancient spinster aunt who was bedridden. That's how it had always been. Generations living together, sharing the same roof and the same meals. It was certainly more economical. It was safer and kinder.

Suad turned up her nose at the retirement village. She explained to the estate agent that she was an honoured member of her son's family. She was the most important person in the house. Everything she wanted, she got. Her preferences were respected, and her wisdom was appreciated. She was cherished.

'That's wonderful for you,' smiled the estate agent. 'You must all be very close.'

'Yes,' said Suad. 'I've been here four months now and I don't want to go anywhere else.' But Suad still missed the city. She missed being able to go out without needing a lift in a car. She missed the company of friends her own age. When would the countryside start to feel like home?

Chapter 8

For Eid that April, Suad bought the family a coffee machine. This was for the adults. She gave money to the children, as was the tradition. Crisp notes which they found delightful. Hamza said that all children would soon have bank cards or use their mobile phones. Cash would be a thing of the past. Suad could not visualise such a future. 'I will be long gone,' she said. The thought was a relief. The world was changing around her, little by little becoming unrecognisable. Everyone older than her or her own age was passing away. The film stars of her youth and the world leaders who made the news. Being old wasn't just about the physical decline. It was slowly not belonging, not knowing the people around you, not being in the centre.

Sometimes she said things and no one replied. She had so many memories and young people didn't have enough time to listen. They were all so busy. She found herself repeating stories. She spoke too long until she noticed that the person she was speaking to was eager for her to stop. It was awkward. Apart from the regular phone calls with Najla, there were not many people she could talk to anyway. More and more people were using texts. They would text and ask about her. She would rather they called. They did on the anniversary of Sherif's death. One whole year. Was she less in pain, less lonely? His death was not a shock anymore, but it still felt recent.

Suad fretted about her flat in London. Hamza had promised that they would go to London together and organise it. He had promised to take time off work, but he never did. There was always one thing after the other. Work trips, Zahra's sister getting married, the roof needing repairs. It was one excuse after the other. In the meantime, Suad was unsettled. Sherif's things were not yet tidied away or given to charity; that wasn't right.

It had not been nice, the way she left her home. She needed to finalise her affairs in London. She had not said a proper goodbye to her flat before rushing off to Mazen, then to Nesrine, then coming here. All with a small suitcase. She wanted her things. She didn't want to shop for anything new. She didn't want to borrow or keep wearing and washing the same clothes. She resented having to buy new things to wear when she already had enough in London. Perhaps she could go alone, give up on Hamza and just do it herself.

When she suggested this to him, he was appalled. 'No, just be patient. Next month I promise. I will take time off and we will go together.'

Her neck was bothering her. The pain from the old work injury flared up. Lots of pain that she kept to herself. On good days, that weren't so windy, she went for walks. The walks were good for her body, but she felt all alone. No neighbour to say hello to or exchange a few words with. She started to sing to herself. Sounds she knew from childhood, songs she hadn't heard for a long time. One day she searched for some on YouTube. To her delight they were there.

She fell ill in early summer with flu. She took to bed and tossed and turned with fever. She dreamed of Sherif and that made her happy. The dreams came one after the other, one leading to the other. In the dreams, she was not surprised that Sherif was nearby. She forgot that he had died.

Zahra looked after her once again. She took time off work and drove her to the doctor. Zahra was most attentive, making her hot drinks and making sure she took the antibiotics on time. It crossed Suad's mind that Zahra was happy that she was ill. Zahra found it natural that Suad was weak and bedridden. The elderly should need some help, but not be a nuisance. They should be grateful for every small thing. The elderly should work their way towards death without complaining.

Suad's recovery coincided with the start of the warm weather and the school holidays. The children spent the long sunny days at summer camp and then went to stay with Zahra's parents in Manchester. Suad missed them. Without them, her days stretched long and empty. The night prayer was at 11.00 PM and the dawn prayers were at 2.00 AM. Unless the sky was cloudy, it never became completely dark. Twilight hovered all through the night. Suad found her sleep disrupted. After staying up late to pray, she found that she couldn't sleep again. By the time she had finished praying and got into bed, it was time to get up at dawn again. Zahra and Hamza told her that there was a special dispensation for children and the elderly to pray at an earlier time. It was not compulsory for her to stay up. But she wanted to.

One night, at midnight, she parted the curtain and saw the countryside spread under a gentle light. It was such a beautiful sight. Strange and attractive. She quietly put on her coat and shoes and stepped outside. She sat on the garden bench. It was cold in a nice way and the air was fresh. Slowly, very slowly, the sky around her turned from dark grey to lavender. She lifted her face to catch the first ray of sunshine. Peace, beauty, she felt part of the harmony of life. The next night she took her prayer mat with her and prayed the dawn prayers in the open air. It was as if she was moving in time, becoming young again. Sherif was near her, as well as her parents. She was here in Scotland, but she was also with them, surrounded by their love and carrying it on.

Not wanting to face disapproval, she kept her nightly adventures to herself. Hamza and Zahra prayed in their own room and never noticed. Suad tracked the weather forecast in case of rain. She prepared her clothes. There was never a disappointment. It felt right that she was outside, grounded. Once in the middle of praying, she sensed a pair of eyes looking at her. Startled, she saw a fox. She continued to pray, and the fox stood still. It was as if the fox understood what she was doing. Then it went away and she was safe.

Now that Suad was up most of the night, she slept in late. She would wake up at lunchtime. By the time she ate, tidied up, caught up with the news, made some calls, it was almost time for Hamza to come home from work. She no longer had heavy empty days stretching out ahead.

Zahra noticed this change on the days she was working from home. 'You've turned day into night,' she said with disapproval. 'You're not depressed, are you? Auntie, you must stop drinking coffee in the late afternoon. It's the caffeine that's keeping you awake. One morning coffee is enough.'

Suad ignored her and continued drinking coffee in the early evening. Zahra confiscated the coffee pods. When she woke up at noon, Suad would find one coffee pod near the machine. The rest were all hidden away until the following day when she was entitled to another one. One pod a day. That was her ration. And she had been the one to gift them the coffee machine! This was bad enough but then her nightly outings were discovered too. Hamza and Zahra were angry.

'This is not normal behaviour.'

'It's not safe!'

'Sneaking in and out in the middle of the night! Why are you acting so strangely?'

They started putting away the kitchen key. Suad was locked in at night. Her freedom was curbed. She was widowed and old, but her own son and daughter-in-law were treating her like a difficult teenager.

Chapter 9

Although Hamza and Zahra stopped Suad's night-time wandering, they did have several treats for her. A day trip to Loch Ness and then, when the children came back from Manchester, a family shopping trip to Inverness to buy new school uniforms and supplies. A month later, Zahra took Suad with her to the first parents' evening at the school. Hamza agreed to look after the children. Suad and Zahra would dress up, have dinner in town and then visit the school. Zahra bought Suad a new autumn coat for the occasion and a new headscarf. She even offered Suad some of her make up, but Suad refused. She no longer wore widow's black but putting on makeup was a stretch too far.

The dinner was a success. Zahra was kind and attentive. She spoke about things that interested Suad. She also spoke about her own parents and siblings, who Suad knew well. The food was reasonable, as far as restaurant food went. Suad would have liked to have dessert after the meal, but Zahra was in a hurry to get to the school on time.

They saw Maha's teacher first. Her name had a 'Mrs' before it and she was sturdy with streaks of grey hair. The teacher said lots of good things about Maha. Maha was doing well. She was above average in all her subjects. She was polite and had lots of friends. Zahra brought up Maha's weight and asked if her daughter was being teased by the other children. The teacher looked very stern then and said that Maha's weight has never been an issue. Maha was a popular girl who enjoyed games and sports. Suad was happy with this. It was good that Maha had such a sensible teacher. Suad had always believed that Zahra was making too much fuss about Maha's puppy fat.

Things didn't go so well with Yousef's teacher. The teacher, a young Miss something with a nose ring, spoke about Yousef's continuing difficulties with maths. She said that she had noticed a slight recent improvement. However, she still recommended that he remain in the bottom maths group.

'No,' said Suad. 'You need to move him up. You need to push him and challenge him.'

The teacher seemed shocked that Suad was even speaking. Her eyelashes flickered at great speed. Instead of answering Suad, she continued to speak directly to Zahra. 'Are you especially wanting Yousef to move up a level?'

To Suad's dismay, Zahra said 'No. He will struggle, and this will affect his confidence.'

'Nonsense,' hissed Suad. 'The teacher just said he is improving! Move him up. It's a chance. Move him up.'

Zahra's face went tight. She gripped Suad's arm hard, as if to warn her.

But what was the point of bringing her here if her opinion didn't matter? Suad thought. She stopped speaking to the teacher, but she found it hard not to mutter to herself.

The meeting ended and Zahra strode ahead. Suad struggled to catch up. Surely Zahra wasn't intending to leave her behind!

In the car, Zahra didn't fuss over her as she usually did. She didn't make sure that Suad's clothes were safely tucked in before the car door was closed. She left Suad to close her own door. She didn't even help her with the seat belt.

Zahra didn't speak. She gripped the wheel as the car glided down the dark narrow country roads. Suad felt nervous and this made her talk faster than normal. She expressed her approval of the school and how well-organised the parents' evening was. Maha's teacher was mature and sensible. However, Yousef's teacher was a child. Zahra didn't even roll her eyes at this last sentence or utter a protest.

Suad continued the attack on Yousef's teacher. 'She should put him in the higher maths group. She doesn't care. All she's probably thinking of is her boyfriend and her holidays. I've been helping him. I've bought special maths games and I help him. I didn't tell you before but I'm telling you now.'

Zahra didn't even turn to look at her. Suad became even more irritated. 'I don't understand you. You're an accountant. Your husband is an engineer. Unless your son gets a good grounding in maths, he will never get a good job. You say you don't want him to lose his confidence, but he won't thank you in the future when he's earning less than everyone else. Children take their own time to develop. Your duty is to encourage him, push him, put pressure on him. Not just sit back and accept that he's weak.'

This time Zahra snapped. 'Auntie, please stay out of this!'

What was that supposed to mean! 'You mean mind my business? He is my business. He's my grandson.' Zahra was being unreasonable.

The following days were bizarre. Zahra ignored Suad. She barely said hello. Hamza was also aloof. While Suad was having a shower, her room was raided. The abacus, the multiplication cards, the chocolates she had saved for Maha were all taken out. They were dumped on the kitchen counter. Why? So that she could see them and feel ashamed?

An air of disapproval hung around the house. Dinner times were cold. No one laughed or teased. Zahra got up from the meal early. Hamza was cold and distant. The children avoided Suad. Whenever she spoke to them or moved to hug them, they seemed stiff and confused.

On Saturday, Suad's favourite day of the week, the usual routine was disrupted. Instead of Hamza and Suad going into town for a coffee while the children had their swimming lessons, Suad was abandoned at home. Much earlier than usual, before she was even dressed, the whole family went into town without her.

Suad phoned Nesrine. Instead of sympathy, she got a lecture on how she must stop interfering and respect Zahra.

'I do respect Zahra,' Suad said.

'No, you don't, Mama. You must respect her wishes.'

'Her wishes are wrong!'

'You're in her house. You need to follow her rules. Don't you get it?'

What was Suad meant to get? That she was just meant to smile all day. Agree with everything. Be grateful. What was she now? A poor relation. A charity case. This wasn't necessary. Sherif had died while still working fulltime and, as his widow, she had received a generous lump sum. She was also entitled to his pension which equalled his monthly salary. Suad did not need Hamza and Zahra to keep her. She was financially independent. She could be the one helping them.

On Sunday as she was getting ready to cook the falafel, Hamza came into the kitchen. 'You don't need to cook,' he said. 'We are going out to eat.'

'Oh,' said Suad. 'Where are we going?'

He avoided her eyes, 'I am taking Zahra and the children for a pizza,' he said. 'I'll bring you something.'

They had always loved her falafel. Every Sunday. It was a family ritual. A special brunch. They had always said that it was better than any takeout. And now they were going out without her, when the whole family knew that Suad jumped at every chance to go into town.

While they were out, Suad phoned Mazen. He knew already. Hamza had filled him in.

'Poor Hamza,' said Mazen.

'What are you talking about!' said Suad. 'I'm telling you they're ignoring me as if I'm nothing. As if I'm an insect.'

'It's cabin fever,' said Mazen.

'I'm not ill.'

'Cabin fever means the three of you are under pressure because you are stuck together in an isolated place.'

Suad liked what she was hearing. It made perfect sense. This countryside living in the middle of nowhere was the root of the problem. No bus close by. No local mosque. No neighbours to speak to. On the following day, she telephoned the estate agent. That nice friendly girl with red hair, who had told her about the residential village. She invited her over.

Chapter 10

'Behind our backs, you had an estate agent come here!' Zahra was certainly talking to her now. She was pacing up and down. It was the angriest Suad had ever seen her.

'Yes,' said Suad. 'For an evaluation. I want you to sell this house and move closer to town. I can help with the extra money to buy a bigger place.'

'No,' said Hamza. 'We are not doing that. Come on, Mama. Please for the sake of peace.' He sat next to her and put his arm around her. 'Don't be difficult. You should have spoken to me first. Admit you're wrong. Say sorry to Zahra.'

Suad shrugged his arm off. 'I have nothing to apologise for.'

Zahra sighed and sat down. 'Auntie, how could you! Without telling us. Our own house?'

'It's just an estimate,' Suad said. 'Then you would have a better idea of how much you could afford. And I will help, now that the money from your father has come through.'

'I don't want your money,' said Hamza.

'You don't have to be rude,' said Suad. 'I would be more independent if we lived in town. I could go out.'

Zahra interrupted her. 'We always give you a lift whenever you ask to go into town.'

'I don't want to have to ask,' Suad said. 'Also, it's better for the children if we move. There is nothing for them here. They need to attend mosque school, to have proper Islamic Studies. They need friends like them. Look ahead. In just a few years they will want to go to the cinema and go shopping. On their own.'

'I decide what is best for my children,' said Zahra.

'You don't *know* what is best for your children.'

Zahra lips tightened and she folded her arms across her chest.

'Listen,' Hamza said. 'You had a total stranger come to the house without telling us. That's not right.'

'Moving or not is our decision,' said Zahra.

'It has nothing to do with not affording a place in town,' Hamza added.

Zahra raised her voice. 'We decided to live here. It's our choice. It's our house. We like it here.' She was trembling.

'What if *I* don't like it?' said Suad.

'Then you should leave,' said Zahra.

Suad gasped. 'You're kicking me out?' She looked at Hamza. He was as shocked as she was.

'If you're not happy here,' Zahra said in a low voice, breathing out each word. 'If it's not working out between us. Then yes, you should leave.'

Suad stood up and went to her room. Did she walk steadily? She was not sure. Everything felt strange. Like time and distance and place were not normal. She left the door of the guest room open and sat on the bed. She could hear Hamza and Zahra talking but she could not catch their exact words. Hamza's tone was even. It sounded as if Zahra was upset, and he was comforting her. He should be raising his voice, shouting at his wife for kicking Suad out! He should be taking his mother's side, like a real man would do. Sherif would have done that. Suad would never have said anything against his mother.

Suad stared at the door. She expected Zahra to come and apologise. She would grovel and cry. Suad waited, determined to continue the quarrel if need be. She would give Zahra a true piece of her mind. She sat still until she needed the toilet. She could not put it off any longer. Her insides were wobbling. In the bathroom mirror she looked hideous. This was not who she was. This was not the woman Sherif had loved. She changed her mind about Zahra. She would forgive her. She would be grand and gracious. Suad walked back to the guest room expecting to find Zahra. No one was there.

Maybe Hamza would come instead of Zahra? Maybe Zahra was too ashamed to face her. Yes, that was it. Hamza would come and beg forgiveness on his wife's behalf. Then Suad would pile blame on him too. After all, he was not without fault in this whole shameful episode. Knowing Hamza, he would make excuses for Zahra. He would tell Suad something intimate like Zahra is grumpy because of period pain.

She could now hear the preparation sounds of dinner. The door of the microwave. Maha setting the table. Perhaps one of the children would come and call on her when dinner was ready. This sometimes happened when Suad was on lengthy phone calls. Though usually at dinnertime she was in the kitchen, getting in Zahra's way.

Suad waited. The smell of the food wafted through the door. She closed it. Perhaps Hamza would come now with a plate of food. Perhaps Zahra would relent and bring her a plate of food, or send one of the children. Nothing. She opened the door. The family had finished eating. She could hear the plates being cleared away.

Because it was time to pray, Suad prayed. Or at least, she got through her prayers. Her mind was jumbled. She was not angry, she was shocked. She walked around the room. A sound came from the corridor. She opened the door to see Yousef walking from the bathroom into his room. She gestured for him to come over. He ignored her, ducked his head and closed the door behind him.

Her grandson had closed the door in her face. It hurt. It hurt more than anything Hamza and Zahra had said. Like a violent scratch to her core. A child believing his grandmother was a troublemaker. A nuisance. Ungrateful. What was in the children's minds now? In their imagination they would be casting her as a monster. Someone who was harming their mother.

Suad lay down on the bed. She put her hand on her stomach. She should eat something. What was she meant to do? Wait for them to sleep and then sneak into the kitchen? Perhaps they had left food for her at the door of her room? She got up, opened the door and looked. Nothing.

Time passed. She stared at the ceiling and went back over every word Zahra had said. It was not planned. Zahra had not intended to kick her out. Something had happened in the middle of the conversation. Something evil and now a line had been crossed. There was no going back.

Suad needed to think. If she had a bit of food in her stomach, she would be able to think properly. They were starving her. If they could starve her, they could do anything. Suddenly, she felt a rustle of fear. She was afraid of them. Yes, afraid of her own loved ones, her own flesh and blood.

Suad did not know what to do. Now? Tomorrow? For the rest of her life? Sherif would have told her what to do. Her parents would have given her good advice. They were all gone. And her own children were no replacement. Their own lives and families would come first. Their jobs and children were more important than her. There had been a time when Suad was important. Now, she was not.

The house was quiet. They had all gone to bed. Really, Hamza was having a good night's sleep while his mother was hungry and miserable! Suad could not bring herself to go to the kitchen. She fumbled in her room for something to eat. She found a packet of nuts. Nuts were no longer kind to her teeth, but she ate them anyway.

Chapter 11

Suad must have slept because she dreamed of Sherif. For the first time ever, in a dream, she had no doubt that he was dead. She was sure of it and shocked that she could see his outline in the next room. He had no business being here among the living. Yet he was here in Scotland, in Hamza's house. She was stiff with fear, terrified of his ghost. A blast of frost filled the room. She woke up shivering, her heart pounding.

The house was quiet. It was dawn. Suad got up, found her way to the bathroom, came back and prayed. When her heartbeat became steady, she went to the kitchen and drank some water. The dream made her alert. Yesterday's quarrel and the rejection from Hamza, Zahra and the children throbbed in the background. Her mind was on the dream. She had truly lost Sherif now. Even in a dream she could not pretend that he was still alive.

Back in bed, Suad tossed and turned, listening for the sounds of the household waking up.

Would Hamza come and check on her? Would Zahra attempt a quick apology before she went to work? Suad strained, listening for the knock on the door. Nothing. When they were all gone, she dozed off. Then, with a start, it occurred to her that they might have left her a note. She got up and looked under her door, in front of her room, on the kitchen counter. Nothing. Perhaps a text message? She switched on her phone. No new messages.

It was obvious to Suad what she must do. First, she had breakfast and a much-needed cup of coffee. Then she went back to her room and started to gather her things. To think that when she had first arrived the whole family were in the room helping her unpack! Zahra bustling about deciding where Suad should put each item. Hamza darting in and out with an extra blanket, a box of tissues – every little thing Suad could possibly need. Yousef cuddling next to her, chatty Maha sitting on her bed.

Suad was going to leave. Packed, dressed, food in her stomach. She put on her coat and her shoes. She stepped out into the cold, overcast day. She prayed for strength.

Suad rolled her suitcase down the country lane. Why had she not ordered a taxi? Taxis rarely came to the middle of nowhere, to this lonely, ridiculous place. When they did come, they charged the earth. She decided to walk to the bus stop instead. She walked and walked, relieved that it was not raining. She walked on, grateful that her back didn't hurt and her breathing was normal. Her bag made a noise, dragged over this country road that had no pavement. A car passed by. It did not stop. Why should it stop? Elderly people did things on their own. They were not helpless. She was not helpless.

She walked and switched the suitcase from arm to arm. The road was uneven, sometimes sloping down and sometimes with a little incline. But at least she was not going to get lost. There was one road, going in one direction. At last, she reached the bus stop. There was no one else waiting – a bad sign. She must have just missed it. There was a timetable online, but Suad hadn't checked. She stood waiting.

It was time for a snack. She deserved a treat for getting this far. She stood with the taste of KitKat in her mouth, worrying that it would rain. There was a drizzle. She could survive a drizzle. She tried to sit on her suitcase, but it was uncomfortable. There was nothing at this bus stop, no bench or protective roof. She had been warm from the walk but now she was cooler. Not exactly cold, not yet, but she would be, soon. What if the bus never came?

At last, at last, the glorious bus. Suad waved frantically for it to stop. She would not take any chances. Oh, the relief of scrambling aboard. One 'thank you' after the other for the driver who helped her with her suitcase. She didn't understand his accent, but it sounded as if he was saying something kind. She was on the way, warm and comforted by the presence of other people. The bus was slow, stopping here, there and everywhere. Finally, they reached the train station. People, shops, coffee, throat lozenges. She would be okay. She was going home. She bought a ticket and checked her handbag for her house keys. Her house, not anyone else's. Her house which no one could force her to leave.

It was comfortable on the train. The rush of countryside going past her window gave her confidence and she dozed. She got off to change trains at Edinburgh but the large station bewildered her. There were so many platforms, where should she go? She got lost and missed her connection. It was an hour until the next train and it felt like a long hour. There were no benches to sit on and the suitcase was awkward to steer. Finally, her train was announced, terminating at London Kings Cross. Just the word 'London' and tears gushed down Suad's face.

Suad told herself that she was not weeping with self-pity. No, just tears of relief that she had made it that far. It was late afternoon now, the children would be back from school. Her absence would be noted. When her telephone rang, she was not surprised. Hamza was calling but she was not ready to talk. She did not want to explain herself, not before she reached London. Text messages, a voice message. 'Where are you?' That was an easy question to answer. 'On the London train just leaving Edinburgh.' She typed.

'We need to talk,' Hamza texted.

'I can't talk on the train,' she typed back.

Nothing further from Hamza.

Instead, a message from Mazen, 'Are you heading my way? Don't. You can't stay with me. I am right in the middle of moving.'

Another message came in from Nesrine. 'Mama what have you done! Zahra is really upset.'

It was time for Suad to take control of her own life. She would learn to be independent. Her children were busy with their own lives. After Sherif's death, Suad had thrown herself at them and that had been a mistake. The children could not compensate for their father's absence. She was alone now. She was over seventy and had never been responsible for herself. First it was her parents, then her husband. From her father's house to that of her in-laws and then with Sherif in London. Always cared for, protected, guided. She had wanted the children to do the same for her. They had tried, hadn't they?

She had gone to them one by one – Mazen, Nesrine, Hamza. They had welcomed her. They had opened their own lives to her. They had shared. But something went wrong in each case. She did not belong to them like she thought she would. They did not take her advice as Sherif had done. Times had changed, the children had been brought up in another culture. They were not patient enough to put up with her. And she was not flexible enough, not grateful enough. She sent them each a short text, letting them know that she was okay and on her way to London. Then she put her phone away. The train was taking her where she must go. To start afresh. To live alone. To do whatever she wanted to do with the rest of her life.

Chapter 12

Everything in the flat in London was as Suad had left it sixteen months ago. She switched on lights and walked through the icy rooms. Instead of melting into its familiar embrace, she saw everything with a critical eye. The flat suited the old Suad, the one that had been Sherif's wife, but not his widow. She was different now, more compact. She did not need so much. Sherif had been the adventurer and she the cautious one. But now she'd had her own adventures too. She was ready to take risks. The rooms felt cluttered, worn-out, old-fashioned. The furniture she had insisted upon, the odd jobs Sherif had neglected, the curtains she had saved for. Every little thing was a slice of their life together. What they had valued and what they had wanted to get rid of but never got round to. She would have to tidy up. Give things away. Throw out a lot.

But not now. It was too late. Tomorrow. Now she must put the heating on. Now she must sleep. She did not want to sleep in her own

81

bed, in the room she had shared with Sherif for decades. Instead, slowly, carefully, she pulled her bag downstairs into Nesrine's room. In bed, still shivering in her coat, she felt the smallness of the room around her, the feeling of being buried under the damp ground. She must not think of the comfortable room in Hamza's house and the beautiful Scottish views. She switched on her phone. Nothing from the children. No, 'are you there yet?' or 'hope you've arrived safely.' It didn't matter. She was too exhausted for anger and disappointment.

Suad thought she would spend the following day in bed recovering. Instead, she was full of energy. She found porridge in the kitchen cupboard, tea and powdered milk. She peered at the expiry dates of tins of beans, soup and tomato sauce. Almost all of them were fine. There was rice and pasta. It made her happy that she was well stocked. She would need to go out for cheese, yoghurt and vegetables. She would need to stock the fridge for one person. Small quantities otherwise they would go bad. She must shop with an eye on the expiry date. Every item would be for her, what she wanted to eat and not for anyone else. How strange that would be!

Suad already felt that there were too many

rooms. The three bedrooms downstairs had a door down the corridor which led to the garden. This was beyond the needs of a single person. The cost of heating would be high, and she did not want the responsibility of the garden.

She remembered it was Friday and so she went to the mosque. Sherif had preferred walking, but she now took the bus. When she got off, she saw Najla and her husband Bilal walking ahead. Najla looked like she had put on weight and Bilal, even from far away, looked dishevelled. He veered towards the men's entrance and Suad caught up with Najla. Najla gave her the warmest welcome. It felt so natural to walk in together, to sit and then to pray. It was as if Suad had never left. Indeed, some of the ladies she greeted had only vaguely noticed that she had been away.

'I'm back now,' she said. That was all she needed to say. No explanations or admissions of failure. This was her rightful place.

Afterwards, she sat with Najla on a bench in the park across the road from the mosque. They had sat there together so many times. Suad waiting for Sherif. Najla waiting for Bilal. Today they sat for a long time, Suad filling Najla in with all that had happened to her in Scotland.

'You should take in a lodger,' Najla said. 'In

the mosque newsletter there is a Moroccan PhD student who is searching for a place. Call her.'

Suad hadn't been keeping up with news of the mosque. She promised Najla she would look into it. Living alone was not economical. What was enough for one person, could easily be stretched to two or even three. Perhaps she could rent out the master bedroom and offer the student cooked meals? She would then have company and an income. It was worth thinking about.

Najla started fretting about her husband. Bilal was late coming out of the men's section of the mosque. She phoned him and Suad heard Bilal say, 'I'm on the bus. I'll be home soon.'

Najla rose from her seat flustered. 'He forgot we came together,' she said, laughing it off. 'I'd better go so he is not at home on his own.'

After Najla left, Suad went back to the mosque. She caught the last of the food sale in which all proceeds went to the mosque. She bought herself a box of chicken biryani. This could last her two days.

She must get used to coming home to an empty, silent house. No one was there to greet her when she turned the key. This was not easy. The television helped fill the emptiness. Sometimes a creak would startle her. Sometimes she would fancy that there was an intruder, and she would go tight with fear. She locked and double-locked the door. She went around making sure every window was closed that night. All these irrational fears had to be fought and beaten.

The good thing was that Suad was busy and had no time to brood. In Nesrine's old room, which was now hers, she found an unused diary. A pretty, girly notebook. It looked like an unwanted gift from an old school friend. Suad began to write 'to-do' lists for her first week back. They helped her organise her thoughts.

She listed the contents of the house that she didn't need anymore. Were there things that could be sold? She made a separate list for what she could give away and what should be thrown out. Could she do this on her own or would she need help?

It was best to start on her own and see how things went. She began with Nesrine's room. She took photos and sent them to Nesrine. Nesrine didn't want any of her old clothes. Suad was free to keep them for herself or give them away. She found a burkini that Nesrine had hardly worn. It looked almost new. The burkini was made up of three pieces – a swimming cap, black leggings and a long-sleeved lycra tunic. The tunic had a pattern of bright green palm leaves. Suad tried it on and looked at herself in the mirror. Why not? She liked what she saw. When was the last time she had gone swimming? Never in this country. Not since she was a child. Decades ago. But the memory of the warm water was vivid, the memory of floating and turning.

The telephone rang. It was Nesrine. 'Why are you doing this now? Wait until I come and I will help you.'

This did not seem realistic to Suad. Nesrine also wanted to talk about Zahra and how hurt she was by Suad's behaviour. 'After all she's done for you!' Nesrine's voice was full of reproach. 'You just stomped off without a goodbye.'

Suad did not want to talk about what happened with Hamza and Zahra. She could not bring herself to say, 'they threw me out.' The humiliation of it. And the days leading up to it. The feeling of being trapped and the family's disapproval of her. She did not want to explain or defend her actions. Besides, she was in the middle of a new project. She was clearing up the house. True, the children should be helping her. But they were busy in their own lives. She understood this now and her feelings of resentment were fading.

There was so much work! Suad paced herself

and took breaks. She tried not to dwell on objects and all the memories they carried. So many years had passed since she'd bought the fancy tablecloth. It was the one that she spread out when dinner guests came – Zahra's parents and the new imam when he was first appointed. She could even remember the dishes she had served.

She found a jigsaw puzzle in Mazen's room. It had a hundred pieces. She spread out the puzzle on the dinner table. That evening, she worked on it, little by little, starting with the edges. Concentrating on the pieces relaxed her mind, stopped it from wandering towards dark thoughts.

That night, she phoned Najla to tell her that she had called the PhD student. 'She sounded very pleasant. I would like her as a lodger but she has a husband. He's in Paris, she said, but would visit her from time to time. I don't feel comfortable with that. A strange man in my house. I would rather not.'

Najla's voice was flat when she replied. It made Suad ask, 'are you alright? Is everything okay?'

Najla sighed, 'Bilal put his phone in the sink. I think it's damaged now.'

'What made him do that?'

'He's not well, Suad. He's been diagnosed with dementia and it's getting worse. We haven't told anyone. We thought no one would notice little things here and there. But now I am on the lookout all day long. It's like having a toddler in the house!'

Suad remembered how Bilal had forgotten Najla at the mosque and gone home on the bus. She comforted her friend as best as she could.

Chapter 13

A few days later, Suad had reason to congratulate herself. She had finished sorting out the kitchen and the living room. A charity had come and taken away a whole settee, the large dining table with its six chairs, a filing cabinet and a chest of drawers. They had rejected one side table because it was scratched and another because it was stained. No matter. It was still an achievement. Now she could sit with a mug of herbal tea and enjoy all the extra space around her. Never mind the dust on the floor. That was tomorrow's work.

She knew that she was leaving Sherif's wardrobe for last. She hadn't yet gone into 'their' bedroom, even though her clothes were in there too. From Nesrine's room she had telephoned her old friends, the ones she hadn't seen at the mosque. 'I am back home,' she would say and catch up with their news. She told them she was sorry she had been selfish and not checked in on them properly over the past eighteen months. She chatted to her friends, surrounded by Nesrine's old stuffed toys, schoolbooks and photos. It was a girly, comforting space.

Her phone rang in a break between calls. It was Najla, sounding breathless. 'Bilal's not well. He's not well!'

Suad could hear him shouting in the background, banging a door as if Najla was in a room he couldn't enter.

'I'm hiding in the bathroom,' Najla said. 'He's accusing me ... I can't believe it. He accused me of adultery!'

This was completely out of character. The story Najla managed to tell was distressing. Bilal had been watching a football match on television. He then accused Najla of having an affair with one of the players.

'The idea is now in his head,' Najla was distraught. 'A kid on TV! First, he was in tears. It broke my heart. I kept telling him it wasn't true; I wasn't going to leave him. Then he lost his temper. And I became afraid. I don't know what to do. He's punching the door.'

'I'm coming over,' said Suad.

She got dressed and headed out. A long time ago, when she worked as a nurse, Suad had come across such cases. At the time she had found it amusing. Now she knew better. Suad found herself acting as a professional again. Her whole body became alert, ready to pick up signs, ready to assess and take decisions.

Najla and Bilal lived on the nineteenth floor of a high-rise building. It was Bilal who buzzed her in and opened the door of the flat. He was in his pyjamas with food stains down the front. His eyes were vague, but he remembered Suad. 'Where is Najla?' she asked.

'She's gone,' he said, tearing up. 'No loyalty at all. I'm ill and she's run off.'

Suad noticed that his hand was bleeding. He must have injured it when he punched the bathroom door.

'Najla,' she called out moving towards the bathroom door. 'I'm here.'

Bilal followed her. He had forgotten that Najla was in the bathroom.

Najla came out. She looked exhausted and there were dark shadows under her eyes. The roots of her hair were white and the rest a blaze of henna. Najla looked at Bilal, wary and tense. He started to shout. 'I'll never divorce you! No man can take you away from me.'

Najla started to make soothing noises. 'I'm not going anywhere,' she said. 'I'm here. Who told you I want a divorce?' She took her husband's arm and led him to the sitting room.

Noticing his cut, bleeding hand, she started to fuss. This seemed to please Bilal. He relaxed at his wife's concern. Suad went to the kitchen and came back with a basin full of warm water. Najla started to clean Bilal's wound. It looked deep.

'It needs stitching,' said Suad. She started to talk to Bilal. 'You need to go to the hospital.'

He felt in his pockets. 'Someone has stolen my bus pass and wallet,' he said.

'No, they're here,' Najla said. She got up, opened a chest of drawers and brought the wallet to Bilal. He snatched it away from her. 'Thief,' he mumbled and lashed his arm out. She moved back just in time. Bilal's eyes were full of hostility towards Najla. He turned away from her.

Suad could tell that Najla was deeply hurt. There were tears in her eyes. She sat next to her friend and Najla whispered to her. 'Is that him? Is that Bilal? Forty years and he never even raised his voice at me. What happened to him?' Bilal was hunched over the contents of his wallet, slowly checking that everything was in place.

Suad squeezed Najla's shoulder. 'Come, let's go and sit in the kitchen.'

Najla was reluctant to leave her husband,

even though she was only going into the next room. 'I didn't offer you anything to drink,' she mumbled to Suad. Even at a time like this, she felt obliged to be a hostess.

'I will make us a cup of tea,' said Suad. She made Najla sit at the kitchen table and then put the kettle on. Najla twisted her chair so that she could watch Bilal in the sitting room. He was still fiddling with his wallet.

'I don't know what to do,' said Najla. 'How to manage him. I don't want the children to see him like this.'

Najla and Bilal had two sons. One lived with his family close by, but the other one was in Dubai. Long ago, when Najla and Suad used to spend hours in each other homes, the children playing together. There were outings to the park and mosque school at the weekends.

'Your boys would want to know,' said Suad. 'You can't keep this a secret.'

Najla sighed. 'Even now. You say he needs stitches. But I don't want any doctor to see how bad his dementia has become. I'll never let him go into care. Never. Never.'

Suad stirred milk into the tea. 'There are medicines that can help him. He needs to be seen, Najla.'

Najla sipped her tea. It was very hot, but she

93

seemed not to mind. Suad waited for hers to cool down.

'It's a burden I must bear,' said Najla. 'A test for my faith.'

'And you'll be strong and patient,' said Suad. She had always known that Najla was more religious than her, more observant and educated. Now, it was true, Najla was going through a difficult test. Suad remembered Najla's support when Sherif died. On the days Suad was reeling from the shocking loss, Najla had comforted her.

'Bilal wasn't so bad,' Najla was saying. 'Even a fortnight ago, he was fine. Sort of cute in the way he forgot things. We laughed about it, and I didn't mind the extra work. But now, the accusations. The suspicion! It's like he's someone else. I'm sick with anxiety. He goes out and I don't know where he is. Yesterday he was up and down in the lift, not sure whether he was going out or coming back home.' She gave a little harsh laugh and took a sip of her tea. 'Now his phone is ruined. It was a blessing being able to phone him. I tried putting it in a bowl of rice but it's still not working.'

When they finished their tea, Suad said, 'we can all three go to the hospital together. How about that?'

They had to wait for a long time to be seen at the hospital. Bilal didn't lose his temper. He was polite to the staff. When they first spoke to the receptionist, he remembered his date of birth and address. This delighted Najla, but soon she became impatient with the waiting. 'Please go home,' she said to Suad when it was past midnight. 'I would feel better if you did. I'll let you know how we get on.'

When Suad woke up at dawn to pray, she checked her phone. There were several voice messages from Najla. She said that Bilal had acted bizarrely and aggressively when the doctor examined him. After his hand was stitched and bandaged, they had to wait for the specialist on call to see him. She recommended that Bilal be admitted.

Suad phoned Najla. She found her teary but calm and accepting. 'They were lovely at the hospital, very understanding, very gentle with him. They cared too about me, my health and safety. I called the children straight away. Their father is ill and they should know about it.'

'That's good,' Suad said. 'You need their support. And now you need to sleep. You've been up all night.'

'I'll pray and then sleep,' said Najla. 'Thank you Suad. This was the worst day of my life and you were there by my side.'

Suad had not only been a helpful friend, she had also been the nurse she was years ago. She had not lost her skills. She had not lost her confidence.

Chapter 14

Despite the difficult night, Suad was up early the following day feeling calm and grounded. The flat was bright with winter sun and she was full of gratitude. How lucky she was! She had not lost Sherif like Najla had lost Bilal. Forever, Sherif would be fit and healthy in Suad's memory. She would always remember him loving her and trusting her. Nothing had happened to soil this picture she had of him. He had died a clean death. A shock for sure. But there had been no mess, no day after day heartache. And unlike Najla, she had not needed to lie to her children. Even though Najla knew that Bilal was ill, she would always remember how he had accused her of adultery and theft. No matter how hard Najla tried, she would not be able to forget last night. Suad had indeed been spared something terrible.

Suad moved around thanking Allah Almighty again and again. In this mood of grace, she entered the room she and Sherif had shared.

She opened the windows, and the room looked beautiful. A room that was full of happy memories. Full of the warmth and love they had shared. Full of lively conversations and the times they prayed together. Tears flowed down her face, but she did not feel sad. She felt full of life. A life spent well. A life lived fully. She had no regrets, no disappointments. Yes, the children could have done better by her, but she did not hold any grudges.

She called them one after the other to update them with her news. She told them that she had decided to sell the flat and move somewhere smaller, suitable for one person. Nesrine was emotional. She had not said a proper goodbye to her childhood home. Then she started to rant. 'You never liked my husband. You were always against Mo, not matter how hard he tried to please you.' Suad neither agreed nor disagreed. She was sorry that Nesrine was upset. She wanted her daughter to be happy and enjoying her new baby.

When she spoke to Hamza, he said, 'Zahra is hurt. She tried so hard to make you comfortable. She did everything she could, and you just left without saying goodbye. Why haven't you called us before now?' He listed all of Zahra's sacrifices. Suad asked to speak to Zahra. They had not spoken since Suad left Scotland two weeks before.

Suad apologised to Zahra. She thanked her for all that she had done, for all the care and attention. Zahra had indeed done her best. Suad could not deny that. They had not seen eye to eye but they would always be family. Suad could have shown more appreciation; she could have been more fair. Suad's apology sounded formal. Pride stopped her from sharing her hurt and disappointment. Pride stopped her from saying how much she missed her grandchildren. Instead, she tried to explain to Zahra her need to learn to live alone and start a new life. She explained how it had not been easy because she had relied on Sherif for so much.

Zahra sounded put out. Her tone of voice was of someone wronged. 'After all I've done for you,' Zahra sighed. 'What will people think of me!' Suad did not care about what anyone thought of Zahra. She was weary of all this.

Suad had to spend an hour on the phone convincing Mazen to come and help her with the house sale. He agreed but ended up being more of a hindrance than a help. Suad found herself cooking his favourite meals and running around collecting used mugs and plates.

Mazen became a teenager again, spending

most of the morning in bed and the rest of the day on his PlayStation. He had worked hard through his final year at Medical School and felt entitled to a decent rest. Suad had to beg him to take unwanted things to the skip. He did not accompany her when she viewed prospective flats. That hurt though Suad pretended it didn't. It was clear that the children were fed up with her. After all she had given them freely, naturally, her health, milk and years of devotion! Now they could only give her grudging attention and conditional love.

Dogs, cats and penguins looked after their young, she thought. It was humans who needed to be told, 'honour your father and mother.'

One morning, Suad gathered up her courage and went swimming. Modest swimming was held once a week at the local pool. On those days, the pool was reserved for three hours for women and there was a female lifeguard. Dressed in Nesrine's unwanted burkini, Suad walked carefully towards the pool. She was afraid she would slip. All the other women seemed younger than her. Mums with babies, schoolgirls and middle-aged women. What was she thinking! She felt her face grow hot. Were they all looking at her or what it just her imagination? It was too late to go back now.

Besides the water was there, welcoming and waiting for her.

Gripping the railing, she climbed down the stairs into the water. She took her time. The water was warm and pleasant. Her feet felt solid on the pool floor. The water seeped through the burkini and ruffled the material. She walked further into the pool, heading towards the deep end, until the water reached her neck. She pushed the floor with her feet and found herself laughing out loud. It was wonderful to surge through the water.

Suad floated on her back, held up as if she had no weight or cares. It was as if she were a child again. She had not forgotten how to swim. The memories came back. She swam a few strokes and then stopped. She slapped the water with her hand. She wanted to play. She didn't want to swim laps. Not today. Next time. There would certainly be a next time.

Later in the changing room, Suad came across the lifeguard. 'The last time I went swimming was fifty years ago,' she said.

It was fun to see the surprise in the lifeguard's eyes. 'I would never have guessed! You looked perfectly at home in the water,' she said.

Chapter 15

Within months the flat was sold. Suad moved into her new home at the end of the summer. She had loved it from the first visit. It was sunny and warm. It had everything she wanted. Most important of all, it was above ground level. From the window, she could see highways and the sky, the busy streets and the shops. There was a café where men sat outdoors smoking shisha. There was a school where parents gathered at the gate. When Suad was at home, she watched them all from her window. Most of the day, though, she was busy popping in and out.

The building had a lift which was useful when Suad was carrying shopping. Sometimes she used the stairs, and it was good that she didn't need to climb too many steps either. The flat was close to a bus stop, close to a supermarket and not far from the mosque. It had one bedroom, but Suad bought a sofa bed in case a family member needed to spend the night. The living room was large and the kitchen had plenty of storage space.

She spent hours choosing the curtains and they were the exact shade that she wanted. It was a lovely surprise to get a 'Happy New Home' card from all the family. They had also pitched in for a gift card. This was a joy for Suad. There was so much she needed for her new kitchen. She enjoyed buying dishes and cutlery. She had thrown out all her ancient pots and pans and now it was time to replace them with new ones. Smaller ones, of much better quality. Colourful new mugs and tea towels. All her previous ones were stained and worn out. Her old oven gloves were scorched and full of holes. It was time to treat herself to new ones. After stocking her kitchen cabinets, she was proud that her kitchen was now just as well-equipped as Zahra's.

On the day Suad moved in, she met her neighbour from across the landing. Frances, also an elderly widow, had moved in just two days before Suad. The two women navigated the new building together and figured out the complex rubbish disposal system. Frances was tall and held herself straight. Suad judged her to be about the same age as she was. 'You look like an actress,' Suad told her. This made Frances blush. She confessed that she had, when she was younger, wanted to become an actress. Instead, she had worked in an admin role in the theatre and was now retired.

Suad told Frances that it was her first time she had ever lived alone. Frances was surprised. 'Then you must be very brave,' she said. 'They say "learning something new" boosts our emotions and keeps our mind active.'

This made Suad laugh. She did not think of herself as brave. Several times each night, she went around checking that she had locked the door and windows. Sometimes, on hearing a creak or sensing a change in the air, she would get jittery. She was unable to sleep without a night light.

Frances had travelled and lived alone. She had been married twice, both times it was brief. The first marriage ended in divorce. The second marriage left her a widow. She was childless. 'But my goddaughter has a wonderful son,' she said. 'You will see him because I look after him two days a week. I am something of a fairy godmother!'

Suad did indeed see him. The little boy was lively and curious. Suad's flat fascinated him because its layout was identical to Frances's, but all the furniture was different. 'Doesn't he eat?' she asked Frances. 'He's skin and bones.'

'He's vegan,' said Frances. 'It takes him ages

to get through one meal.'

Suad was shocked. 'Not even eggs or milk! Give him a chicken drumstick. Every child loves holding onto a chicken drumstick.'

'I follow his parents' wishes,' Frances said with a shrug.

'You're sensible,' said Suad, thoughtfully.

Frances was a keen walker and she invited Suad to join her. Keeping up with Frances was not easy. Besides, it seemed that Suad did not have the right shoes for walking. This was remedied by going out shopping for new trainers.

The two of them walked along the canal. They spoke of grandparents born a century ago. They remembered outdated fashions and skills that no one now needed. They could remember different names for places and countries. Vanished borders, vanished regulations, old currencies and new illnesses. They spoke of their troubles with glasses and hearing aids. Most of their life was over. Things could all suddenly go wrong – a hard fall, a bad blood test, a broken hip, pneumonia. But that was even more reason to take pleasure in life. The smell of flowers, a silly joke or the taste of ice cream.

In the family WhatsApp group the children posted videos and photos. The videos were delightful. Suad could hear her grandchildren's voices and see the expressions on their faces as if she were with them. Plans were being made for Mazen's graduation next year, though it was still several months away. Nesrine and her family were coming over the UK from Indonesia. Hamza and his family were coming from Scotland. It had been ages since they were all together. After the graduation ceremony, the whole family would go for a fancy dinner at a restaurant. Suad was looking forward to this family reunion. She would show the children how different she had become since they had last seen her. Independent and capable.

Mazen was keen for Suad to buy a new outfit for his graduation. Several messages and photos of outfits passed between them.

'I want you to make a good impression,' said Mazen.

Suad became suspicious. Mazen's classmates would be at the graduation as well as their parents. Her son was now an eligible bachelor.

'Why?' she asked him. 'Is there a girl you want me to meet?'

'Maybe,' Mazen replied. He was in high spirits. 'Maybe. But I'm not ready to answer any questions. The graduation is still a few months away.'

Months away or not, Suad would be prepared.

A possible girlfriend graduating at the same time as Mazen! Her parents would be there and Suad would meet them. It would be casual and friendly. Suad would not let Mazen down.

It was time for a shopping spree. This time she would really treat herself. She chose a purple dress with flowers and a matching purple satin jacket. The colours suited her.

Chapter 16

Suad was happy when Najla came over to visit her new flat. Najla gave her a potted plant as a gift. 'It's a lovely flat,' Najla said. 'You are doing well, Suad.' The swimming had improved Suad's appetite. It gave her face a healthy glow.

Because of Bilal's illness, Najla now belonged to a carers' support group. 'I gave a speech,' she told Suad with pride. 'I spoke to a room full of people about Bilal. I explained to them that he was ill because Allah loved him and wanted to cleanse him from all his sins. I think they understood.'

Najla was learning ways to manage Bilal's condition. She was learning breathing exercises which she now taught Suad. Suad, with her new trainers and brisk walks, tried not to appear smug. She dragged Najla with her through London's beautiful parks. 'Bilal doesn't know he's in London,' said Najla. 'He is not with me here. He's back home. Yesterday he talked for a whole hour about his childhood. He talked about his older brothers who fought in the war of liberation. He talked about foraging in the woods. I never knew any of these things. He spoke clearly and didn't make a single mistake. It was a joy to listen to him.'

Frances wanted Suad to teach her how to cook falafel. They would be the perfect festive vegan Christmas brunch. The lesson ran into difficulties. Suad did not have a recipe. She had learnt to cook by watching her mother. She used her eyes and nose.

'How much?' Frances would ask.

Suad would reply, 'a little.'

'For how long?' Frances would ask.

'Until the smell comes out strong,' Suad replied.

In frustration, Frances dashed to the library, just before it closed for the holidays, and borrowed three cookbooks on Middle Eastern cooking. The two spent time comparing the directions in the cookbook with what Suad did.

From Najla, Suad learnt Sudoku and how to play Solitaire on her phone. From a helpful member of staff, she learnt how to manage the self-service checkout at the supermarket. From Frances, she learnt how to use Google Maps. She taught herself how to use an air-fryer.

Living alone meant that she had to do

everything for herself. Every choice concerned her and no one else. Because Suad was not used to this freedom, it took a long time to find out what she did and didn't like. Days were long and the winter evenings were even longer. More time to watch old films on YouTube, more time to devote to prayers.

Before Suad knew it, winter was over and it was Ramadan again. For the first time in her life, Suad fasted alone. She had no family to share the pre-dawn meal with and no one to prepare treats for. Instead, every afternoon she walked to the mosque. At sunset, the mosque served a communal meal and that was where Suad broke her fast. It was fun to sit on the floor with the other women, a plastic tablecloth spread out with dates, cups of water and fruit. After prayers, there was a hot meal and then tea and coffee. Suad stayed on for the night prayers. That was when the prayer hall filled up.

She returned home on the night bus. By the time Suad got to bed it was midnight and time to set her alarm for the pre-dawn meal. After that she slept in late. Her day felt short. There was just enough time for a shower, minimum housework and then it was time to walk to the mosque again. Suad barely had time to talk to her children. In the family WhatsApp group she said she wanted to celebrate Eid together. Hamza pointed out that they would all be together soon for Mazen's graduation. Two trips south would be too much. Suad was upset at first but agreed that it made sense.

Ramadan was not always easy. But the discipline and working towards the end of month celebrations made Suad feel a sense of purpose. She loved to hear the beautiful nightly Qur'an. She was living a life that was smooth and full of meaning.

Frances, who Suad only met briefly on the landing for the weeks during Ramadan, was impressed by the daily fasts. 'This is proof that no one is too old for anything!' she said in awe. Suad, although groggy from staying up late and deprived from caffeine, was proud to explain the benefits of fasting.

On the morning of Eid, she slept through her alarm and missed the Eid prayers. She woke up and the room was full of daylight. Suad looked sadly at her best scarf hanging over the armchair. She had taken it out to air, as she hadn't worn it for a long time. Disappointed, she continued to lie in bed. She had been looking forward to the prayers. They always lifted the sadness that Ramadan was over. They gave a stamp of approval to the relief that one could eat all day again. She could now have coffee in the morning. She could now join Frances on the walks that she had no energy for while fasting. She switched her phone on to a flood of Eid Mubarak messages from the children. There were videos of the grandchildren speaking directly to her, showing off their new Eid clothes. There were emojis of cakes, balloons and cookies.

Her first Eid in her new home. She would make it special. First, the smell of coffee wafting through the flat. Suad heated up a cinnamon bun in the microwave. The two aromas were a pleasure as was the taste in her mouth. Later if the weather was still nice, she would text Frances and join her for a walk. She could wear her best scarf too, why not? But first, she put on the television. She would watch something silly today. Something fun to make her laugh.

The doorbell rang. Suad got up and moved cautiously to the door. It could not be Najla, she was with Bilal today. Who else could it be? Suad gave a gasp of surprise when she peered through the spy hole. Hamza, Nesrine and Mazen! Her three children, here for her! She thought she would not see them until Mazen's graduation. How lovely and well-dressed they looked!

They exchanged hugs and kisses. Their voices and warmth surrounded her. Every one of them, the same children they had been long ago. The babies she had held in her arms and pampered. Only Suad knew their essence and what could never change. Of course she forgave them, she would always forgive them, no matter what. She felt the thick bonds of blood all around her, her eyes filling up. Oh, she could have dabbed on some perfume. Really, she could have baked Eid cookies, at the very least. 'What am I going to do with you all now! I have nothing to give you,' she said.

They weren't listening. They were putting flowers and food on the kitchen counter, moving and taking up space, puffed up and proud of themselves for being good children. She would be better prepared when she met up with them again next week at Mazen's graduation. She would be wearing her new purple dress and a little bit of makeup. She would talk about all her activities and about the swimming – perhaps one day she could even go swimming with Yousef and Maha! Zahra would be there too and Suad would make up with her – all water under the bridge, all forgiven and forgotten. But for now, her three children filled her flat. Their voices were loud. Their bodies big. She stepped back as Nesrine handed her a present, insisting that she must open it now.

Mazen and Hamza cheered when Suad finished unwrapping the gift. It was a picture in a beautiful heavy silver frame. A photograph of Suad and Sherif, one that Suad hadn't seen before. What a wonderful surprise! In the photograph, Suad and Sherif looked happy and smiling, dressed up for a celebration. Suad could not remember what they were celebrating. It might have a been a birthday? But the photograph was taken at night and usually all the children's parties were in the afternoon. She looked again, then she remembered. It had been taken one New Year's eve. The old year stale and the next one beckoning, fresh and promising. That was when the photo was taken. They were welcoming in a new year.

About Quick Reads

"Reading is such an important building block for success"
– Jojo Moyes

Quick Reads are short books written
by bestselling authors.

Did you enjoy this Quick Read?

Tell us what you thought by
filling in our short survey.
Scan the **QR code** to go
directly to the survey or
visit: **bit.ly/QuickReads2025**

Thank you to Penguin Random House, Hachette and all our
publishing partners for their ongoing support.

Thank you to The Foyle Foundation for their support of
Quick Reads 2025.

A special thank you to Jojo Moyes for her generous donation
in 2020–2022 which helped to build the future of Quick Reads.

Quick Reads is delivered by The Reading Agency, a national
charity with a mission to empower people of all ages to read.

readingagency.org.uk   **@readingagency**   **#QuickReads**

The Reading Agency Ltd. Registered number: 3904882 (England & Wales)
Registered charity number: 1085443 (England & Wales)
Registered Office: 24 Bedford Row, London, WC1R 4EH
The Reading Agency is supported using public funding by
Arts Council England.

Find your next Quick Read

In 2025, we have selected six
Quick Reads for you to enjoy.

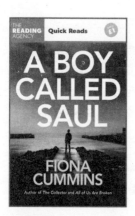

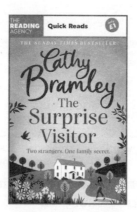

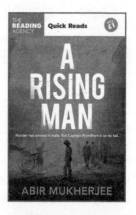

Quick Reads are available to buy in paperback or ebook and to borrow from your local library. For a complete list of titles and more information on the authors and their books visit: **readingagency.org.uk/quickreads**

Continue your reading journey with The Reading Agency:

Reading Ahead

Challenge yourself to complete six reads by taking part in **Reading Ahead** at your local library, college or workplace: **readingahead.org.uk**

Reading Groups for Everyone

Join **Reading Groups for Everyone** to find a reading group and discover new books: **readinggroups.org.uk**

World Book Night

Celebrate reading on **World Book Night** every year on 23 April: **worldbooknight.org.uk**

Summer Reading Challenge

Read with your family as part of the **Summer Reading Challenge: summerreadingchallenge.org.uk**

For more information on our work and the power of reading visit: **readingagency.org.uk**

More from Quick Reads

If you enjoyed the 2025 Quick Reads
please explore our 6 titles from 2024.

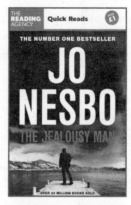

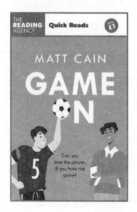

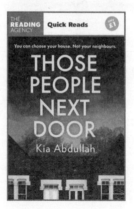

For a complete list of titles and more information
on the authors and their books visit:
readingagency.org.uk/quickreads

ALSO BY LEILA ABOULELA

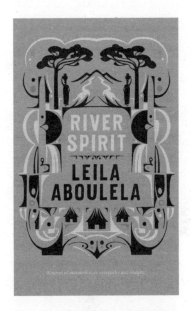

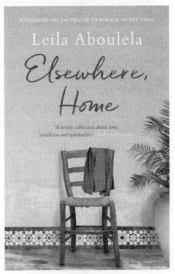

SAQI BOOKS

Gable House, 18–24 Turnham Green Terrace
London W4 1QP
www.saqibooks.com

First published in Great Britain 2025 by Saqi Books

A full CIP record for this book is available from the British Library.

ISBN 978 1 84925 073 3
eISBN 978 1 84925 074 0

The EU GPSR authorised representative is Logos Europe,
9 rue Nicolas Poussin, 17000 La Rochelle, France.
Email: contact@logoseurope.eu

Printed and bound in Great Britain by
Clays Ltd, Elcograf S.p.A

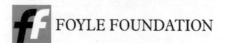